Notes From The Grooming Table

DOGS

Rabbits

CATS

BETH PHILLIPS

To order additional copies of this book, contact:
Xlibris
844-714-8691
www.Xlibris.com
Orders@Xlibris.com

ISBN: Softcover   978-1-6698-0526-7
        EBook   978-1-6698-0525-0

Print information available on the last page

Rev. date: 12/29/2021

Chapter Outline

Dog skills test

1. Problem solving skills:

A Timing for uncovering treats under a can. 3-5 seconds. Above average.

Pet sitting:

1. It was my experience to get bonded and find a name for my pet sitting business which I named Beth"s Bowwows and Meows. Clients were found by advertising in a local flyer and joining a local business association. Car signs and business cards were helpful as well. Pet sitting contracts were used to document current medications and key arrangements.

2. Some of my experiences included one day visits to overnight stays. Current pricing was obtained for local areas. These pet sitting jobs were not limited to only dogs. Some were cats and exotics. One client even included a beta fish and an iguana.

3. The local animal shelter volunteer experience taught me too use soft leashes and neighbors and experience taught me to avoid the retractable leashes.

4. Also some pet sitting experiences require beyond the usual activities to involve giving medications. This information can be obtained by the pre- pet sitting visit by taking a proper fully filled out pet sitting contract before the actual provision of services begins.

5. Also it was important to know who or whom would have keys to the property besides myself. For example, one clients brother also had keys to the house.

6. Additional duties can include watering plants and adjusting lights. Their are many different types of methods of entry including physical keys and alarm systems

Dog Grooming:

1. The dog grooming experience included a trip to the local dog grooming school. There i learned the different dog breeds and were tested on my knowledge of them. Also the hands on experiences of the sanitary cuts, the ear cleaning and the nail trims. Best practices are to use cotton balls for the ear cleaning until they come out clean. It is suggested to keep them to show the client for groomer accountability. Deciding to set up a dog grooming business in the garage was the likely decision. Dog tables and a dog bath were installed. A hot water heater also. Occasionally one thing would have to be unplugged to use another piece of equipment. The dog bath required a permit and inspection. A Security platform was installed to see clients arriving and greeting them.

2. The costs for setting up a home garage dog grooming business run around $6000- $8000.

3. The local trade shows for dog groooming are fun in the sun workshops in Orlando. Many new ideas can be generated by attending these trade shows.

4. Also grooming neighborhood dogs was discouraged by a neighbor.

5. Their were many different dogs with challenging behaviors which required modifications including diversion tactics and desensification tricks.

6. Dog report cards are available but for my clients they didn't seem to excited to receive them. Other forms include vet referral cards.

7. For example, dogs who did not care for the drier or the baths were rewarded with treats when they would make contact with the drier or the bath. Their was one dog in particular named Riley who did not care for the drier at all and would try to bite the dryer. This required a great deal of patience and thinking out of the box. For me, drying the areas that did not offend them worked best. Several dogs did not like the bath and required two people to get them in there. One could use treats to get them up the stairs.

8. Being certified as a reiki master was useful also for transferring energy healing to the dogs.

9. Their was one opportunity for grooming a rabbit.

10. The rule for dog collars is the two finger rule. The collar should be loose enough that two fingers can fit between the collar and the dogs neck.

11. Dog grooming businesses require a business license that must be renewed each year. Also insurance in which I used Governors Insurance.

12. Dog grooming skills are also a great skill to offer nearby animal shelters.

13. On one occasion I groomed a German shepherd for the Hillsborough County Animal Service later named Pet Resource Center.

14. An EIN was obtained and various paperwork including articles of incorporation. One time I neglected to complete these forms and was fined.

15. Also giving away free coupons for local shelters special events. One particular event was the humane society Tuxes and Tails. In which one year later the purchaser did contact me about redeeming.

16. Contracts with local rescues also increase business and reputation.

17. Dealing with the loss of a long term client in terms of your dog grooming client pet transitioning to the next life. This was very difficult for me and on a few occasions resulted in the shedding of tears.

18. It is always good to have a good rapore with a local vet that you feel comfortable referring business. Some vets will return the favor and refer business to you and some will not.

The Shelter Volunteer Experience.

1. The Shelter Experience for me was photographing pets available for adoption and dog grooming. Also one included pet a pet program where family dogs were taken into assisted living facilities to visit patients.

2. I always had a natural inclination to brush the pets and an innate ability to feel their pain.

3. Volunteer coordinators come and go. Since the inception of my volunteer experience their has been three different volunteer coordinators. I was told that the door would always be open to me.

Canine assisted therapy.

1. It was my experience that the various facilities needed shot records. The pets had to be evaluated the director of Canines for Christ. Most of the people were thrilled to talk about pets that had in the past. Especially those that had pets similar to the one you might bring. One must sign in and sign out of facilities. Also it was suggested that pets increase appetite in the elderly. Also, some of the residents kept treats to give to pets. The pets brought lots of smiles to the residents.

Cat and Rabbit grooming.

My only experience with this was a matted cat that would not let the owner brush and two outdoor matted rabbits.

The dog collar and leashes.

It was my experience to use soft leashes and avoid retractable leashes. Two fingers should fit in between the collar and the dog neck.

Career day demo

On one occasion I was asked to attend a school career day in which I was asked to show the students what a dog groomer does. I brought my dog and did a demonstration of the job requirements involved in the profession of being a dog groomer. Brushing, ear cleaning, nail trimming, etc. Explained to them about leashes, collars, etc.

EQUIPMENT NEEDED

→ Scissors   Thinnin shaver
→ Blades   40   30   15   9   7   5   4
→ clippers   Wahl

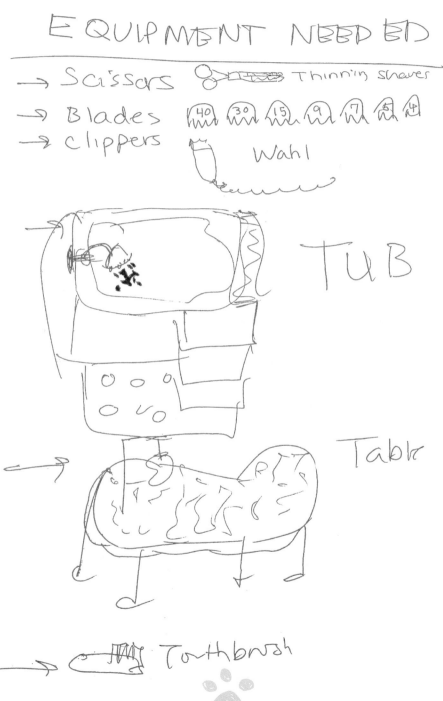

TUB

Table

→ Toothbrush

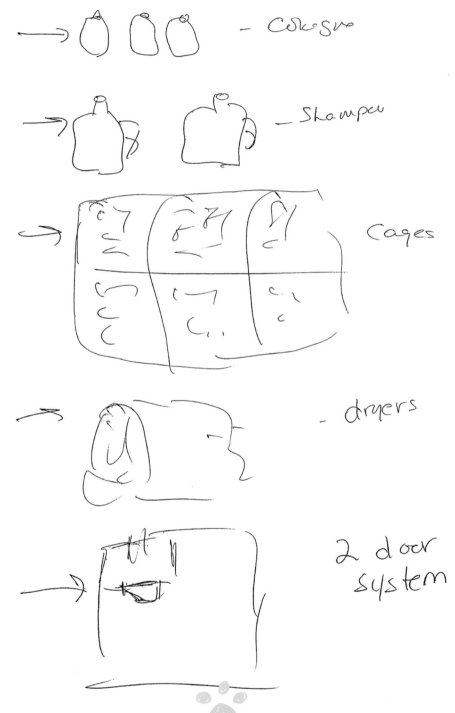

— Cologne

— Shampoo

Cages

— dryers

2 door
system

Desired to have dog off balance keep him up there

Color in the following
Blades and number in
order from shortest
cut to longest cut.

7

40

4

30

5

15

Label the following

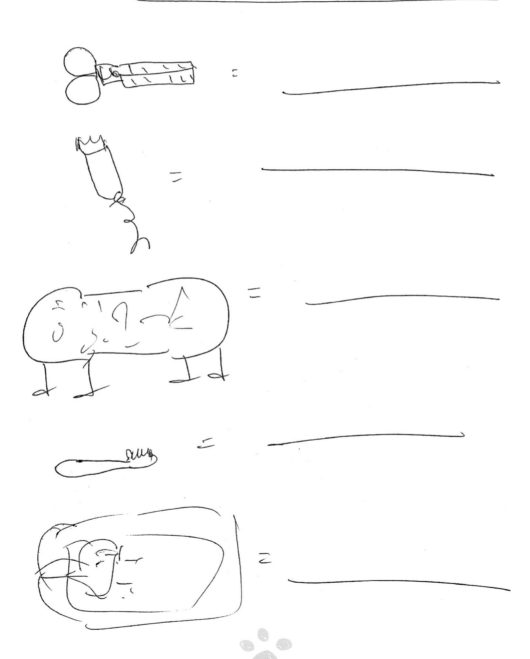

= _____

= _____

= _____

= _____

= _____